LESTER FIZZ,
Bubble-Gum Artist

by RUTH SPIRO

illustrated by THOR WICKSTROM

dutton children's books

The Fizz family had artistic flair.
Winslow worked in watercolors.

Dorothea dabbled in the darkroom.

Cousin Cornell created collections.

Lester Fizz tried to create art, too.

His paintings were pitiful.

His landscapes looked lifeless.

Even his doodles were drab.

In the Fizz Family Museum, everyone,

even the littlest Fizz, had a work of art displayed.

Everyone but Lester.

One day after school, he went to Uncle Edgar's
studio in search of inspiration.

"*POP! POP!*"

"Hello, Lester!"

"Uncle Edgar, how can I become an artist, too?" he asked.
"The way I see it, Lester, anyone can be an artist. Look at this sculpture. What do you see? What *don't* you see? What do you *want* to see?"
Lester looked at Uncle Edgar's sculpture. He thought about what he wanted to see.

Suddenly, a powerful breath rose inside
Lester. His belly bulged. His tongue trembled.
His limber lips labored and his
face turned fuchsia.

Something wonderful appeared.

"Excellent!" cried Uncle Edgar.
"Things are finally shaping up,"
Lester replied.

From that day on, Lester practiced his unique technique.
First, he put on protective gear. Next, he prepared
his gum, chewing until it felt snappy.
Then, shaping the gum with his front teeth,
Lester breathed life into his art.
His belly bulged. His tongue trembled.
His limber lips labored and his face
turned fuchsia.

Then Lester's bubble appeared.
Of course, there were a few disasters
along the way.

In confined spaces,
Lester had to
exercise restraint.

At Fizz family functions,
Lester's bubble-blowing
created quite a buzz.
Most important, Lester
discovered that windy days
were simply too risky.

Still, Lester stuck with it.

Lester's art teacher took note of his newfound talent.

"Tomorrow is our school art contest," she reminded him. "I hope you'll consider entering a creation." Lester was so excited, he thought he might pop. "If I win, my family will see I really *am* an artist," he said.

On the playground, children gave up their turn on the swings just to watch Lester create his bubbles. Some were brave enough to challenge him. Georgia blew a gigantic pink bubble. Lester blew a super-duper gigantic pink bubble.

"Superb!" the children said.

Frida blew a bunch of bubbles.
So did Lester.
"Stunning!" the children cried.

Cousin Cornell blew a bubble shaped like a hot dog.
Lester blew a bubble shaped like Mona Lisa eating
a hot dog, with pickles and a side
of cheese fries.
"Show-off," Cornell mumbled.
"The way we see it,"
said Georgia and Frida,
"he's an *artist*."

Lester popped in a fresh piece of gum and began
his next creation, when . . .

PTHUT!

Out flew his front tooth.
His bubble burst.
The sculpture sank.
"Hsssssss!"
"Now you're just full of hot air,"
said Cousin Cornell.

Hssssss...

"You didn't actually think you'd win an art contest
with *bubble gum*, did you?"
"I gueth I blew it," Lester said. He hung his head,
fearing his career as bubble-gum artist was over.

That night, Lester placed the tooth under his pillow and waited for the tooth fairy. When she arrived, Lester thought she looked like Uncle Edgar wearing a ballet tutu.

"Lester," she whispered, "your new tooth will grow in soon,
but until then, you must continue blowing
your bubble-gum art."
"Remember . . . *What do you see?*
What don't you see?
What do you want to see?"
And with that, she was
swept up by his ceiling fan
and became a pink blur.

The next morning, Lester gathered his gum and packed his
protective gear. He would enter the art contest.
At school, he was greeted by Cornell's toothy grin.
"Chew on this," he said. "I've created a colossal collection
for the art contest, and *I'm* going to win."

Fortunately, Lester had Georgia and Frida
to cheer him on.
"*L, E, S! T, E, R!*
Lester is our superstar!"
This was Lester's chance. His whole family was there.

He put on his protective gear.
He prepared his gum.
Then he began to warm up.
He thought about
what he wanted to see.

Lester tried to blow a bubble shaped
like the Statue of Liberty.
"Bubble trouble?"
asked Cousin Cornell.

Lester remembered the tooth fairy's advice.
"What do you see? What don't you see?
What do you want to see?"
Lester paused to chew on his thoughts, and also
on another tiny piece of gum, which he stuck
in the empty spot where his tooth used to be.
"It's a stretch, but I think I can do it," he said.
"I am a Fizz!"

Lester didn't have
much time.
The judges were
getting closer.
They passed
Pablo's painting.
"Superb!" they said.

They stopped to
consider Cornell's
colossal collection.
"Stunning!" they cried.

They made their way toward Lester.
He took a deep breath. His belly bulged. His tongue
trembled. His limber lips labored and his face
turned fuchsia.
Lester thought about what he wanted to see.
Slowly, slowly, he blew . . .

...the most spectacular bubble ever.

"Stupendous!" the judges declared, awarding Lester
the blue ribbon.
The Fizz family was flabbergasted.
"The winner!" said Winslow.
"A vision!" said Edgar.
"Don't move!" said Dorothea.
Georgia and Frida cheered.
"By gosh! By gum!
Our Lester's gone and won!"
"Show-off," Cornell mumbled.

"The way / thee it," said Lester,
"I am an artitht."

THIS BOOK is about art as much as it is about bubble gum or Lester's quest to fit in with his artist family. All of Lester's friends and family members are based on famous artists from around the world and throughout history. Here's a little more information about them.

The Boat Builders, 1873

Winslow Homer (1836-1910) was an American painter who specialized in maritime art.

Migrant Mother, 1936

Dorothea Lange (1895-1965) was an American photographer famous for her photos of the poor during the Great Depression.

The Dance Class, 1874

Edgar Degas (1834-1917) was a French Impressionist painter famous for his studies of ballet dancers.

The Little Dancer, 1880–1881

Originally a wax sculpture of a ballerina, which Degas dressed in fabric and ribbons, and was later cast in bronze with fabric clothing.

Man in Armor (Portrait of Vincenzo Anastagi), 1571 – 1576

Doménikos Theotokópoulos, or El Greco, (1541-1614) was born in Crete but is known as the first great genius of the Spanish School.

The Pink Studio, 1911

Henri Matisse (1869-1954) is regarded as one of the most important French painters of the twentieth century.

A Sunday Afternoon on the Island of La Grande Jatte, 1884–1886

Georges Seurat (1859-1891) painted with tiny brushstrokes of contrasting colors. His style became known as Pointillism.

Les Demoiselles d'Avignon, 1907

Pablo Picasso (1881-1973) was a Spanish painter most famous for his development of the Cubist style.

Untitled (The Hotel Eden), 1945

Joseph Cornell (1903-1973) lived in Queens, New York. He gathered objects from the street and from flea markets to create his collections.

Jack-in-the-Pulpit No. 3, 1930

Georgia O'Keeffe (1887-1986) is an artist best known for her depictions of the American Southwest and flowers as if seen close up.

Self-Portrait, 1940

Frida Kahlo (1907-1954) was a Mexican artist who painted many self-portraits, which she intended to express her inner feelings.

If you look closely at the art in the Fizz home and Lester's school, you'll see more paintings and art works that inspire Lester's bubble-gum art. In addition to the artists in this gallery, see if you can find references to Mary Cassatt, Paul Cézanne, Leonardo da Vinci, Vincent van Gogh, Claude Monet, Berthe Morisot, Edvard Munch, Auguste Rodin, Jan Vermeer, and more. How will they inspire you?

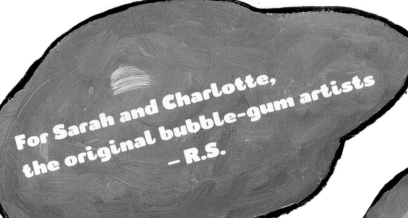

For Sarah and Charlotte,
the original bubble-gum artists
— R.S.

To Eric, Jessica,
Jennifer, Stanley, and
Diane Michelson . . .
my very own Fizz family
— T.W.

DUTTON CHILDREN'S BOOKS
A division of Penguin Young Readers Group
Published by the Penguin Group
Penguin Group (USA) Inc., 375 Hudson Street, New York, New York 10014, U.S.A.
Penguin Group (Canada), 90 Eglinton Avenue East, Suite 700, Toronto, Ontario, Canada M4P 2Y3 (a division of Pearson
Penguin Canada Inc.) • Penguin Books Ltd, 80 Strand, London WC2R ORL, England • Penguin Ireland, 25 St Stephen's
Green, Dublin 2, Ireland (a division of Penguin Books Ltd) • Penguin Group (Australia), 250 Camberwell Road,
Camberwell, Victoria 3124, Australia (a division of Pearson Australia Group Pty Ltd)
Penguin Books India Pvt Ltd, 11 Community Centre, Panchsheel Park, New Delhi - 110 017, India
Penguin Group (NZ), 67 Apollo Drive, Rosedale, North Shore 0632, New Zealand (a division of Pearson New Zealand
Ltd) • Penguin Books (South Africa) (Pty) Ltd, 24 Sturdee Avenue, Rosebank, Johannesburg 2196, South Africa
Penguin Books Ltd, Registered Offices: 80 Strand, London WC2R ORL, England

Text copyright © 2008 by Ruth Spiro
Illustrations copyright © 2008 by Thor Wickstrom

All rights reserved.

CIP Data is available.

Published in the United States by Dutton Children's Books,
a division of Penguin Young Readers Group
345 Hudson Street, New York, New York 10014
www.penguin.com/youngreaders

Designed by Irene Vandervoort

Manufactured in China   First Edition

ISBN 978-0-525-47861-4

1 3 5 7 9 10 8 6 4 2